HANG IN THERE

Published By

HANG IN THERE

Written by Harneet Singh

Copyright ©

HARNEET SINGH - POETRY WORLD ORG 2020

ISBN (Paperback) - 9788194928805

First Edition : 2020

Book Design by POETRY WORLD

HANG IN THERE

HARNEET SINGH

ABOUT THE AUTHOR

Harneet Singh is a 15 years old, 10th class student who always felt that life is full of inspirations. What is required is to be observant. A badminton player, a wonderful orator & a superb cook, he aspires to be a Computer Engineer. He loves to experiment & is very jovial, helpful & hardworking person.

PREFACE

Every nook & corner provides you with something that can inspire and motivate. Open your eyes and you will see, a little ant teaching you 100 life lessons. Even an eagle can inspire you to never give up. When you go through the lines of great men, you will see how they crossed the hurdles & turned adversity into opportunity. The positive outlook which can be developed right from the childhood goes a long way in shaping our personalities.

Hence, a short collection of stories to inspire, motivate & entertain.

ACKNOWLEDGEMENT

Dear God: Hold My Hand And Guide Me

That's the prayer I have been doing since I was two years old. And the Almighty has always been at my side. Every thing I do is because of His blessings. I pay reverence to God Almighty for being kind to me.

It's said that the blessings pour in from Heaven. I have always felt that power of blessings in abundance in my life, thanks to my Dadaji, who keeps an eye on me from heaven itself. I feel he might be bribing God too for all of us. It's him who has always been my biggest support. Although he is not with me any more, he was, he is and he will always be my inspiration.

I take this opportunity to thank my Dadi, Nanu, Nani and Bade Papa for always encouraging me to follow the path my heart desires. Their positive reinforcement never allows me to feel let down or to give up. A big thank you to these pillars of my life.

My parents are my strength. They have supported me on each and every front. They always have my back which in turn gives me confidence to try new things. I express my immense gratitude to them for always being there for me.

It's a proven fact that your biggest critic is your biggest patron too. My elder sister **Sahej** scolds me, fights with me and dominates me all the time. But when it comes to a situation where I stand alone, I just have to turn and look. She as a bullet proof shield is always there to protect and take the brunt. Always appreciating and commending even the smallest effort I make, she is my biggest fan too. I don't say it often but I love you the most didi.

I express my heartfelt thanks to the team of Poetry World Org. for all the help and support.

INDEX

"FIRST MEETING WITH THE GOD"

It was a bright sunny Sunday, 9 October,2003. Me & my friend were playing PUB-G at my home. Suddenly, we both saw black colored smoke and clouds in the blue sky. We both were very startled that how come a clear day had suddenly took a turn about. The sky was covered with black clouds. After two to three minutes, a bright light came through the dark clouds. It was blinding us, we were not even able to open our eyes. After some time a giant creature came down towards us & said, "I AM GOD".

I thought it was just a prank, but my friend agreed to what was happening. So, I asked Him to give a proof of Him being the 'GOD'. He said, "You have annoyed me by asking such a question." He started crying & as He cried rain started. The flow of rain increased as His tears increased. After 10 minutes, my friend asked me to apologize in front of Him, I apologized & asked him not to cry. He stopped crying & the rain also stopped. I also believed in His words that He is God.

We both asked him about His sudden arrival. He replied, "I have come here to have a meeting with two boys named Sidak & Pukesh." We both were surprised that why God wanted to have meeting with us. Pukesh told God that we are Sidak & Pukesh. God said, "I have checked your PUB-G profile & I was shocked to see your performance in that game. He was very happy with our scores in the game. He asked us to have one – one wish each & he will fulfill it. I didn't take much time & asked God to give me a trip to 'LAS VEGAS' for 3 years & at the same time Pukesh said, "his wish was that all his wishes would come true." God thought that his wish was very different. He said, "Your wishes will be fulfilled" & then He returned in the clouds & all became clear.

Next day, my father got a phone call from his manager & was informed that he has got transferred to 'LAS VEGAS' the beautiful country. I was shocked to hear the news & thought that it was only because of yesterday's meeting with the God. Me & my family were settled in 'LAS VEGAS'. And I talked to Pukesh every evening at 7:30 p.m. One day I got a phone call from Pukesh & he said that his wish has also come true. He wanted to be a class topper & he had stood first in the class. He was so happy.

After 12 years, our family came back to India. And I switched on the T.V. & heard only one name - 'Pukesh Ambani' at all news channels, Hearing Pukesh Ambani's name I remembered my old friend, Pukesh with whom I played PUB-G every day. I called my friend many a times but no reply was there. After many futile calls, my phone call connected with his phone. I asked him for a get together. While on the phone call, I remembered that he also belongs to Ambani family & asked that, "Are you Pukesh Ambani, whose interview is being broadcasted in every news channel?" The answer was "YES! I wanted to become the richest man in Asia, I am the richest man in Asia, Do you remember our first meeting with the God? This all is because of that meeting on 9oct, 2003."

I WAS DUMBSTRUCK YET HAPPY.....

"DON'T LET HER GO"

There lived a man named Kishore Verma. He was gifted with a baby girl & gave her name 'Sita'. Sita loved her parents. Sita was a very intelligent girl. Now, when she was in the age where she would get married, she was bachelorette. Sita had completed M.A. & B.Ed in English from a reputed institute in Delhi. Her father always dreamt of going to foreign countries, but due to lack of good education & lack of money, he was not able to fulfill his dream. One of their relatives suggested that Sita should get married. But her father was very selfish & always thought about himself, he thought that he should find a foreigner groom for his daughter & after marriage he & his wife will get settled abroad. He started looking for a good & suitable match for Sita.

One of Kishore's friend, Salman had his relatives settled in abroad from very long time. When Kishore got the news that they are coming to India to find a suitable bride for their son. Kishore started insisting Salman for forwarding the marriage proposal of his daughter to his relative's son. Salman agreed to do so. Kishore invited Salman's relatives to his home. When they reached Kishore's residence. Kishore & his family members found that the boy to be married was not a boy but a middle aged man of about 45 to 50 years of age. His name was Rajan.

Rajan seemed very old for his daughter, to be married. He called Salman aside & refused for their marriage. Salman explained Kishore that it is the only chance for Kishore to go to abroad. Kishore was influenced with selfish motives of his own & was blindfolded by greed. After a day Kishore called his daughter, Sita, & said that he had found a foreigner groom for her with whom she would spend her whole life. Sita refused & said if they would force her then she would commit suicide. Two friends of Sita; Rani and Lakshmi, told the breaking news of that day to Kishore that how, a foreigner married an Indian girl and took all the money from dowry & had never been seen from the last 7 years.

Kishore was taken aback by the news. Kishore discussed the matter with his wife & also told her that if we would force her then, she would commit suicide. Next day, Kishore & his wife talked to Salman & said sorry to Rajan and his family for inconvenience.

Rajan, Salman & others were not happy. They threatened Kishore & his family. But Kishore had now come to his senses and had realized that his greed would ruin the life of his beloved daughter. But Rajan & his son thought it was a huge humiliation & they kidnapped Sita and abduct her when she was alone at home.

This left Kishore & his wife shell shocked. They went to the police and filed a complaint but there was no signature of Sita. On the other hand, Sita was perplexed at first and didn't know what to do. But then after a couple of days, she pretended to have fallen in love with Gabbar (Ranjan's son) and won his trust. When after a week Gabbar started completely trusting her & became careless, Sita knocked him in sleep with a flower vase, took out the keys & ran away.

She reached the nearby police station and narrated her story. Rajan & Gabbar were arrested.

Sita was awarded by the Mayor of the city for her bravery. Kishore blamed himself for all the trouble Sita had to go through & vowed never to be greedy again.

"A HIDDEN TRUTH"

There was a man named Amish Devgan who lived in a city. He had four children. His wife Pratibha named her four children as Sudan, Vatan, Rakesh, Lark and the next day they all four lost their mother in an accident. They were given short names as April, May, June, and July by Amish. When they all were young they played together, they ate together, they even slept together and moreover all four studied together. They all had very lovely and caring, nature towards their father and for each other too.

All five didn't need anything but love and affection. But, a day came when Sudan, Vatan, Rakesh and lark had a fight among themselves. When this bad news reached Amish, their father he was shocked to listen that his four children had a fight among themselves. Similarly their friends, neighbours, relatives were also shocked to listen the same. Some of their friends did not even believe as these four were inseparable and shared a strong bond .No one could even think that they could argue. Amish thought of two ideas, one was to bring them together as before or let them go on their separate ways to avoid everyday quarrel.

He tried his best to make them unite once again, but Amish failed. Then, he thought it was better to let them go. Next day he invested all his property worth Rs 78 ,50,00,000 in shares and due to good luck his all shares got sold out and he had profit of Rs 53,00,00,000 and by this money he started four different business for his children April, May, June and July. Fight between all four increased too much that they even wanted to change their surnames from Devagn to something else.

Sudan chose "Pichai" as his surnames. Vatan chose "Tata" as his surname. Rakesh chose "Ambani" as his surname. Lark chosed "Zuckerberg" as his surname.

Amish Devgan started Voogle for Sudan Pichai, Chota motors for Vatan, Artiance for Rakesh and Pacebook, a social media company for Lark and at present they all four are now CEOs of their respective companies. This truth that they all four are real brothers is only known to their father Amish Devgan and the secret rivalry among them still continues..

"UNSOLVED MYSTERY"

It was a bright sunny day dated June 20,2010 on calendar. I was getting bored in the house as whole of my family was busy. It was quarter past two when I decided to go outside to get relaxed with one of my close friends, Yuvraj. I called him up several times but he didn't pick up my phone call, then I remembered that Yuvraj once told me that he didn't pick anyone's call on Sunday. Then, I tried to call, Aman Dhiman, my bestie & asked to go outside to relax ourselves. He suggested that we must go on bicycle so that our physical exercise would also be done. But, my cycle was not in the condition to be travelled for long distances.

Then, I suggested him to take his bike then he said it has been taken by his father for that day as no other vehicle was available. At last my sister suggested to take the car. Then, me & Aman took my car and started our journey. While on the way, we came across a tunnel. It was dark and we had never seen it before. Aman, who is very adventurous by nature decided to go through the tunnel. Just a mile inside we saw a board which said, "SHORTCUT TO JAPAN"

We thought it was a joke. But decided to give it a try. We started our journey to Japan. After 13 hours of travelling we smelled something very bad as if some animal had died. We both thought that some rat or dog had died and we closed the windows of our car but that smell didn't end up. As gradually, the speed of the car was increasing the smell was also increasing. Then, we stopped near a pond and thought to investigate ourselves. While I was checking our car and I was shocked to see a strange thing which didn't belong to us. I opened the boot of the car and saw a body of a young girl.

We were both afraid to see her & were not able to stand properly. After 10 minutes, Aman & Dhiman gave me an idea to throw this body in the pond and run. I followed his instructions and we both threw her in pond but we kept her driving license, and then we took the way back to home.

Now, after 10 years when it is 2020 the news came with the title 'Breaking News' - "A girl named Kezia has been killed". Her body has been found in the pond between the road way to Japan from India. I was shocked to hear the news and called Aman. We both remembered that we have taken her driving license and matched the picture from news paper and it was the same. Later it was investigated by our local police that she was killed by her own father as she didn't listen to him and moreover she had ran with a boy to get married to him against the will of her father. We were scared that we would both be found and will be punished. And also the mystery of her body in our car was yet to be unfolded.

We were in a fix - should we come clean or stay quiet. The forensic report said, "Kezia was murdered 50 years ago." How was that possible? We had thrown her body just 10 years ago. The whole thing left us perplexed. The mystery was getting deeper and deeper.

If she was murdered 50 years ago, how come her body was there in our car 10 years ago? We decided to research and hired a private detective, Manan Kapeluyzhnji. Manan and his team after 6 months of research found that it was not the first incident when someone had spotted her body in their vehicle. On investigation 5 more people admitted to have encountered the same experience as me and Aman Dhiman had.

This all was beyond understanding. No amount of scientific explanation could be given for such bizarre incident.

An old saint, Chirag Lamba said that, "May be it was the soul of Kezia that was trying to tell the world about her brutal murder."

Were we hallucinating or was what the old man said real?

We don't know!!!

"IF I WERE A BOOK"

I don't want myself to be kept in children's library

But on digital screen(s)

Not because, I hate them or their nuisance

But when they tear my body parts or scribble badly on
my face,

I hate that moment the most.

I want to destroy the ignorance of children,

by giving them courage and knowledge

I want myself to be a surgeon

Or a nurse, saving lives, holding injections of
medicines containing knowledge to impart in
children's mind to make their future BRIGHT.

"THAT DAY"

(JUST FOR FUN)

That day

When I had to pay

For those rice

kept by me with a sigh.

That day

When I had to pay

As a huge clever mice

Ate my bought white rice.

"CAN'T BE DROPPED"

Mohit was the only child and was loved by all. He was well behaved and good in studies. But from last one month he had become careless, rude, aggressive and even got less marks in his tests. His mother did not know what to do. All the laughter and happiness had vanished from their lives. Everyone was now worried about what has caused this drastic change in Mohit's behavior. After a week his parents noticed some positive change in his behavior but it was just temporary and lasted only for a day.

All the members were very scared, they decided to take him to the specialist and a counselor. They all reached the clinic. After seven hours check-up and discussions the specialist concluded that nothing could be done and referred him to PGI for detailed and thorough checkup. Next day, Mohit and his family went to PGI and after four hours checkup the doctors gave Mohit a long list of medicines to take after every four hours.

He religiously took that medicine for almost five months. His family members didn't notice even a little bit of change in his demeanour. Then, to give one more try his parents arranged a meeting with a famous personality Mr.Rupinder Singh. He advised them to consult a counselor whose name was Mr. Varun Mehta. Mr. Varun after talking to Mohit advised his parents to ask Mohit's favourite thing or the thing he likes the most to do.

Mohit's father asked the same question to Mohit and he replied, "I love to play badminton," and Varun Mehta told his parents to let him join the Badminton Academy if they wanted to see the positive change in him. He joined the Academy. Just after a couple of days, they could see Mohit becoming relaxed, cheerful, and disciplined once again. Although the change was slow but it was definitely there.

The game therapy continued and so did the improvement. But Mohit's father was still baffled. 'How could a game do what even the medicines couldn't?' So, he went to Mr. Varun once again and asked him to solve the mystery Mr. Varun explained, "In today's competitive era, the parents and children in their success rat race forget that even our mind and soul needs a break. Hence just a few hours of indulgence in an activity that pleases us can do wonders. So always let your mind and soul take a break and tell them."

"Milte h ek chote se break k baad".

"LEND THEM YOUR EARS"

The day when half of the July had already gone by. It was a windy day and I was listening to my favorite song. I could not hear any one while listening to the song. My mother called me several times but I paid no heed to her. She switched off the T.V. in anger & asked me to bring some vegetables from the market. I took 200 rupees from my mother & took my bicycle to buy vegetables.

While on the way, I met my school friend, Ishu. He is 9 months younger to me. Ishu was teasing a cute puppy. I asked him many a times not to do such kinds of mischief. But he was in the habit of not listening to what others are saying. He didn't stop & he tried to put his finger in the puppy's mouth, Puppy's parents saw Ishu teasing their cute pup. They both ran towards Ishu.

Ishu was so scared and ran at his full speed but due to his bad luck, his bike slipped and he fell on the road and the two dogs came and caught hold of his leg and bit him hard.

As a result, not only Ishu had to bear the pain of the bite but also got 14 injections and had to bear the painful experience 14 times.

From then onwards, he mended his ways and promised not to repeat his mischief again.

"CHASE YOUR PASSION"

Raju was the only child of Mr. Verma who was a CEO of a handloom company. Mr. Verma was a single parent, with no other close relative than his son. His love and pampering made Raju careless & irresponsible. It was not a point of worry when Raju was still a child but as he grew up to be a teenager and didn't learn to value things, relations as well as time, Mr. Verma was worried. He wanted his son to change his ways. But to his horror, this behavior kept on increasing, leading to every day complaints by his teachers, neighbours and acquaintances.

And this irresponsibility also led to Raju's decline in academics. All this negative report became like a thorn in the heart of Mr. Verma and he constantly worried about the future of his son. This constant worry led to the doom of Mr. Verma's business too. Raju and his father were now very poor. Raju failed in his final examination. His father was really disappointed. Raju had to leave the school. Mr. Verma had cancer and was hospitalized. They could not afford the hospital bill.

On one side Raju's father was on ventilator and on the other hand Raju became a street thug and started selling drugs which was not only illegal but dangerous too. They did not have a single rupee now to buy medicine for Mr.Verma's treatment. When Raju's father knew about the condition of his child that he had became a drug smuggler, he realized it was something very bad. He himself complained about his child to the local police and Raju spent 6 months of his life in jail.

When he came back from jail, he was a new person. He realized that he had to earn some money for treatment of his father. He started working as a pizza delivery boy at Dominos and stayed there for 6 years and collected some money. His father saw the change in Raju and wanted Raju to complete his studies. He promised his father that he would be a successful person in future.

One week before annual day celebrations in his college, his father passed away. He decided to give a solo singing performance on 'FATHER'. The chief guest was A.Praak, a famous music director and composer of that time. He found talent in Raju Verma and asked his college director to grant him leave. Director agreed and Raju Verma went to Mumbai with A.Praak where he changed his name from Raju Verma to Armish Verma and worked so hard on his singing skills and launched his first song - 'LE MAI AAGYA' (in punjabi) with the help of A.Praak. And now he has launched so many punjabi songs and has given punjabi industry a new look. He completed his promise to his father that he would be a successful person.

"THIS IS THE PERFECT EXAMPLE OF RAGS TO RICHES"

"THANKFUL PRINCIPAL"

It was a rainy Sunday and I had my mathematics final examination the next day. I studied whole Sunday to get good score in the subject. Before breakfast I studied for about 7 hours then I had my breakfast. After that I continued studying. At 11:00p.m. my friend whose name is Manan called up to ask syllabus of mathematics examination. I was shocked for a moment to listen what he was saying. I told him the syllabus but at the same moment he replied, 'That's why, I am asking you the syllabus. I have confirmed this from teacher, Mrs. Poonam that 2 more chapters are also included in exam.'

I was dumbstruck 'TWO MORE CHAPTERS....', 'How it is possible?' So, I called my classmate, Parth to confirm the syllabus. He also told the same syllabus which Manan had told me, then I put my phone aside and studied whole night and slept at 5:00 a.m. thinking I'll wake up at 6:00 a.m. But when I woke up and saw the time, it was 6 in the evening. It was as if the Earth slipped from under my feet. I cried and cried that how I could make such a blunder. It was really painful for me to digest that I had missed my maths examination. At 7:00p.m. my family came back home from Amritsar. When my father asked the reason why I was crying, I told him the whole story then he said, "Do not worry, I will talk to your school's principal about this." My father called her up and she said that today's examination has been cancelled due to some technical issue(s) and will be rescheduled soon. I was so happy to hear the news. Then I studied for my exam again and prepared myself whole night and again the same happened, I slept and woke up the next evening.

This time, I thought that nothing could be done and I would be declared as a failure. This time my mother called up my principal, as my father was angry with me. Principal said, "It was postponed today also as one of the boys was absent in the whole school." My mother asked who that child was, She replied, "Your ward is that only child". I and my mother apologized in front of principal.

Principal also said that, "School had also made a policy that when any child is absent at the day of examination then that day's exam would be postponed and will be conducted the following day."

"A MAN"

One who eats mouth watering food

Is a man

And one who survives on a dry chappati

Is also a man.

One who is head of a nation

Is a man

And one who is civic in the nation

Is also a man.

One who builds its infrastructure

Is a man

And one who lives and dies in it

Is not anyone else,

But A MAN.

One who steals someone's belonging(s)

Is a man

And one who runs to catch him

Is also a man.

Think several times before hating someone,

As there is only one and single body,

And a soul,

That respires....

"POSITIVE TO NEGATIVE"

The color black

denotes negativity to all

For me as well

A day when our teacher

asked to draw anything with

only color black

Everyone in room ignited their

deep thinking

And, I just painted

my page with color black

and that made me realize

it had become capable of letting the Stars, Moon and
Galaxy shine

with black in it's backdrop

The most beautiful sight.

"UNBELIEVABLE PHONE CALL"

That day when I was making video on TIK-TOK [a commonly used social media application] was very embarrassing for me as I was not able to make that video from a very long time, I was taking re-takes every time. After taking at least 150 re-takes, I learned that song. While learning the song I remembered the sayings of one of my best friend, "When you are not able to complete your video on TIK-TOK, then understand that something would happen good with you in a short span of time." I was very excited. Then suddenly I got a phone call from TIK-TOK CEO- [Bite Dance]

I was hesitating to pick up his call. I picked up the phone call and the conversation among both of us was :---

Bite - Hello! sir.

Me - Hi, Good morning, sir.

Bite - Congratulations!!

Me - I asked the reason.

Bite - Are you a fan of Faisoo [popular creator] a TIK-TOK star?

Me - YES!!

Bite - Do you want to meet Mr. faisoo as you are a big fan of him and has liked his all videos?

I was shocked to listen this. Then, I simply said, "YES'. After 2 days, a message from Bite Dance came that 'When your likes on your videos will be 100M then only you would be able to meet Faisoo. Then, I started my journey to make my likes from 2.2K to 100M. It took me 17 years to reach 78K. I was so excited that, it took me another 13 years of my life to reach to 99M. Then, It was the time when my likes were not increasing from 99M for such a long time.

After 3 days, Supereme Court banned the TIK-TOK application in India because, deaths were increasing due to TIK-TOK. I was shocked to listen the verdict of the apex court i.e. Supereme Court. I cried a lot and thought that I wasted 30 years of my crucial life and didn't work and earn money for my livelihood.

It was 17 July, 2020 written on calender when, I wrote all this in my personal diary...

"SILENT PEOPLE HAVE THE BIGGEST HEART"

Mohan Mittal with his wife and his step mother lived in a small town, Sadulpur, in Rajasthan. Mohan was a small trader who earned money which was hardly enough to meet the basic necessities of his wife and stepmother. His wife, Geeta Mittal was a sad soul as she wanted to see whole world with her eyes, stay at 5 star hotels but on the contrary she was not able to fulfill even the smallest desire of hers. After 2 months of her marriage she had known that she could not get money from her husband and then decided to work independently without telling anybody. She saved her money which she earned from stitching others clothes. After 7 months Mohan and Geeta were blessed with a baby boy. Mohan was not so happy to see his child and didn't find any indication that he would become a good and successful man. But on the other hand his wife, Geeta loved him so much and always played with him and gave him the name, Bhakti Mittal, thinking that he would save her from this life of poverty and slavery.

Years passed, Geeta used to stitch others clothes, Mohan used to earn money from small trade and

Bhakti started going to school. He was an intelligent and good looking boy. He always got good scores in academics and opted commerce in his class 11th. After finishing his school he requested his father that, he wanted to study more and wanted to go abroad. In this case he would need money to get admission in good institute. But, his father was not able to pay the fees. At the same time Mohan had an argument with his wife, Geeta saying, "You are always busy talking to your friends, Where is your contribution?" They tried taking loan from bank but their application was rejected.

Next day, Geeta handed Mohan a black leather briefcase containing all her savings which she earned from stitching others clothes saying ,"HERE IS MY CONTRIBUTION, IT'S 10 LAKHS, I WISH I COULD HAVE GIVEN MORE BUT.....". Mohan appreciated his wife a lot and gave that money to Bhakti.

He went to America and got admission in St. Xavier's college, where he studied a lot to make his dream come true. He wanted to become the greatest steel supplier in the world.

As he was an intelligent boy he is now a CEO of a great steel supplier Company. He is called by name-B.N. Mittal by his loved ones. Now, according to 2011, Forbes list, his personal worth has been recorded as 1st in U.K. and 6th in India. He always gave all the credits to his beloved mother, Geeta Mittal.